A Little Moment
of Me *for:*

. Megan Bird . ♥ .

First published in Great Britain in 2018 by Hodder & Stoughton

An Hachette UK company

1

A CIP catalogue record for this title is available from the British Library

ISBN 978 1 473 69169 8
eBook ISBN 978 1 473 69170 4

Set in Baskerville by Anna Woodbine, thewoodbineworkshop.co.uk
Printed and bound in Italy by Lego S.p.A.

Hodder & Stoughton policy is to use papers that are natural, renewable and recyclable
products and made from wood grown in sustainable forests. The logging and
manufacturing processes are expected to conform to the environmental regulations of
the country of origin.

Hodder & Stoughton Ltd
Carmelite House
50 Victoria Embankment
London EC4Y 0DZ

www.hodderfaith.com

Dear Parents

I have called these books Little Moments *(not* Vast Hours!*) because I want them to be just that. A moment to pause in you and your child's busy day. A moment to step away from the hustle and bustle of life. A moment simply to be still.*

The Bible is full of the most amazing stories, written down by many authors over hundreds of years, all of them inspired to share the story of this wonderful God and his amazing love for his children. The words in this book are not literal translations – they are inspired by verses and passages that I love.

My hope for all my readers, big and small, is that the words and pictures will connect you to the true heart of God and that the truth of who God is and how much God loves you will nestle deep in your heart.

Jenny

Heaven's knitting needles
made me;
tiny stitches
of love put me together.

Psalm 139:13

I am God's

m a s t e r p i e c e.

Ephesians 2:10

Because I belong to God
I am brand new,
inside and out.

2 Corinthians 5:17

I won't live
my
life

in
a
box!

I am free and strong
and full of promise.

Psalm 119:45

Nothing
on the
outside
of me defines who
I am on the inside.

2 Corinthians 3:18

Even before

I began to g r O W,

God knew every detail of

who I was and who

I would become.

Jeremiah 1:5

God made me to be fruitful...

...growing and spreading good fruit everywhere I go.

John 15:16

There's no room for fear
to live in me because
l o v e
has locked it out.

2 Timothy 1:7

I

am

free!

John 8:36

Don't compare yourself
to others; it will be like
wearing clothes that
d o n ' t   f i t   y o u !

Galatians 6:4-6

Use your freedom

to help other people.

Take a moment
to be together and
e n c o u r a g e
one another.

Speak courage
into one another and
champion your friends to
reach for more.

1 Thessalonians 5:11

Throw away criticism,

it will wear

you

down

and bring you sorrow.

James 5:9

Fix your eyes on God
and you will be like a
tree nestled beside
clear streams.

We are accepted
for who we are.
So offer that same
acceptance to
everyone you meet.

Romans 15:7

It is better to do life
with a friend. Help each
other succeed...

...and steady each other
along the journey.

Ecclesiastes 4:12

God looks at you

and smiles and God's

love

is reflected in

your face.

Numbers 6:25

Because of God's love
for us we are adopted into
God's wonderful family.

Your God is

overjoyed

with you and sings a song

of love over you.

Zephaniah 3:17

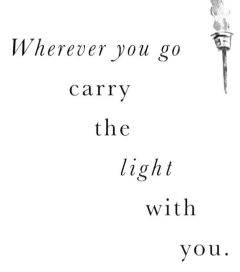

Wherever you go

carry

the

light

with

you.

Ephesians 5:8

Throw off words
that are not bursting
with love and run to the
one who speaks life.

Proverbs 18:21

We are able to overcome
all things because we
are loved by the
one
who
is
love.

Romans 8:37

Don't hide in the dark;

you were created to flourish in the light.

1 Thessalonians 5:5

Because you are loved,
put on the garments of
compassion,
kindness, humility,
gentleness and *patience.*

Colossians 3:12

Draw in close to God and

God will draw you

close into

him.

James 4:8

God is like a strong tree,
stay close to God,
make your home in
his branches and
you will produce
the *sweetest* fruit.

You have been set
free!
Be strong in your freedom
and never look back!